CW00890988

# The Raven's Tale

## and other stories

KENNETH STEVEN

*Illustrations by*
Katharine Wake

SAINT ANDREW PRESS
Edinburgh

First published in 2007 by
SAINT ANDREW PRESS
121 George Street, Edinburgh EH2 4YN

Copyright © Kenneth Steven, 2007

ISBN 978 0 7152 0846 5

All rights reserved. No part of this publication may be produced or transmitted
in any form or by any means, electronic or mechanical, including photocopy,
recording, or information storage and retrieval system, without permission
in writing from the publisher. This book is sold subject to the condition that
it shall not, by trade or otherwise, be lent, re-sold, hired out or otherwise
circulated without the publisher's prior consent.

The right of Kenneth Steven to be identified as author of this work has been
asserted in accordance with the Copyright, Designs and Patents Act 1988.

British Library Cataloguing in Publication Data
A catalogue record for this book is available from the British Library

It is the Publisher's policy to only use papers that are natural and recyclable
and that have been manufactured from timber grown in renewable, properly
managed forests. All of the manufacturing processes of the papers are expected
to conform to the environmental regulations of the country of origin.

Typeset by Waverley Typesetters, Fakenham
Printed and bound by Bell & Bain Ltd, Glasgow

# Contents

The Raven's Tale    1

The Cat's Tale    7

The Lamb    13

The Old Man and the Lark    19

The Nest    23

The Island    29

Lia's New Friend    35

The Fox's Tale    41

The Acorn    47

The Robin    53

The Shoemaker    59

The Present    65

Amy's Christmas    71

# the Raven's tale

When the world was still quite young, a group of animals and birds lived together in a beautiful valley far away. There were high hills up above and sweet meadows running through the valley, and at the heart of everything was a great deep blue river that wound like a snake towards the sea.

There were many magnificent animals and birds in the valley but the most handsome and dignified of them all was the raven. He was a cousin of the crow, but he did not look in the least like his relative. The raven had the finest purple feathers on his tail and a crown of crimson feathers on his head. But  most of all, the raven had the sweetest voice of all the birds in the valley – finer than the blackbird that sings at dawn and richer even than the nightingale in the wood. The raven was a truly splendid singer.

The raven's voice was so famous that birds and animals came from far and wide to hear him. After a while it became a tradition for the raven to fly down to a certain tall rock by the river at seven o'clock each evening. He would sing to his excited audience until the first star came out above the mountains.

This was how they arranged themselves. The stags and deer would lie down closest to the raven's rock. Behind them were the bears and the foxes. In all the little nooks and crannies in between the mice and the rabbits and the ferrets and the moles would gather, and the otters put up their heads from the river to listen. All the other birds perched in the antlers of the stags and had the best view of the lot.

Soon the animals began to bring gifts for the raven to thank him for his wonderful singing. The reindeer would bring soft cushions of moss, the heron brought a mighty salmon, the moles brought worms (which the raven did not care for much), and the bullfinches left him bright ripe cherries. After a while, thanks to all the good food, the raven began to grow rather plump.

One winter the frost came early to the beautiful valley. On the summits of the mountains there was a first sprinkling of snow – they looked like giant puddings with sugar on top. The days were pure blue and the end of your nose tingled when you went out first thing in the morning. Even down at the river there were jagged edges of ice in the rocks.

On Saturday evening, the raven thought that he might be beginning to catch a cold. He looked at his reflection in the deep, cold river water. His gorgeous crimson crown was just as magnificent as before. His shiny black beak sparkled and gleamed – there was no outward sign of a cold. He noticed just the tiniest tickle at the back of his throat. Should he sing that night or should he cancel his performance? He had never let his adoring audience down before. He knew that two golden eagles were flying in specially from a neighbouring valley – what would they say if he didn't sing? If only the rest of the creatures who were gathering could really understand his beautiful voice! He must surely sing for the eagles – they would be so disappointed if they did not hear such wonderful music. They would have heard nothing like it in their valley. He would just *have* to sing.

He swept down on to his rock with pride and shook his purple and crimson feathers. He sang and sang until at last a great crescent moon rose up behind the hills and night flowed into the valley. All the animals shivered with cold as the raven continued for much longer than was usual. But they stamped their hooves and hooted and brayed when his last song was done and they left a bigger pile of presents than ever beside the rock to thank him for his wonderful performance.

Well, the raven waddled off to bed, very pleased and very proud. He didn't believe he had ever given a performance like it before. He had shown them who had the best voice in the world! He slept until the sun was quite high in the sky the following morning – and the moment he woke up he realised that his throat was very sore indeed.

The raven set off from among the jagged rocks where he had his home, down to the river for a drink. He had to be careful not to slip on the stones for they were glittering with frost like new-cut diamonds. The raven went forward to the edge of the water and bent his beak to drink. All of a sudden he caught sight of something. He couldn't see the crown of red feathers on the top of his head. He bent forward and he stretched round but no matter how he looked at his reflection in the river he could see not a sign of his beautiful crown. He stretched round in panic to check his purple tail but all he could see were sooty feathers. He looked just like his cousin the crow!

Shaking and puzzled, the raven took a long, long drink. His throat was so sore it was hard to swallow at all. What if his precious, wonderful voice had been damaged? He decided to sing the first few notes of a song. He stood on a rock, put his feet together, and lifted his beak to the skies.

'Ark!'

That was the only sound he made! In horror he tried to clear his throat and he thought of his very favourite song. That was sure to work, he knew. It was his most beautiful song, the one the eagles had come so far to hear last night.

'Ark! Ark, ark, ark, ark, ark!'

At last the raven realised the truth. He had lost not only his precious red and purple feathers but also the voice he was so famous for. That very day the raven flew away from the valley to the far mountains where it is stony and lonely and wild. He is there to this day, with his sooty black feathers and his croaky throat.

The poor raven. All because he was too proud of his voice. He forgot that God has given many different gifts. We may not all have wonderful looks or a beautiful voice, but that doesn't mean that we don't have gifts too. Everybody is special to God.

# the Cat's tale

On Haven Hill there is a mighty wood of oak trees and ivy hedges and dark secret paths. Almost no one ever finds this place, for it's too deep in bushes and trees. It's here that the animals live – foxes and rabbits and badgers and mice. This is their world and theirs alone. Down below Haven Hill is Greenwell Farm with its cows and sheep and tractors and people.

The family that lived at Greenwell Farm had a ginger cat by the name of Rowl, and all the rabbits and mice of Haven Hill feared him like no other creature. They knew that Rowl was a killer. The stories of all the terrible things he had ever done were whispered from mouse to mouse and from nest to nest, winter after winter.

One day in early spring, when the first daffodils shone along the lanes like golden trumpets and trees were turning green with new leaves, the mice decided to go for a picnic in the field in front of Haven Hill.

Everyone had to help for there was lots to do. They sat up the night before preparing things and working out how they would reach the field.

Very early the next morning, before it was light, the mice were up packing little baskets of food with all their favourite things. When they were ready they set off from Haven Hill in a long line, singing songs as they went. The sun was starting to rise like a great red apple over the tops of the eastern hills and everywhere there was the colour and life of spring.

Once the sun was up and they had got down to the edge of the first field the mice played hide-and-seek by the riverbank. They ran and played until they were completely tired out. They went down to the shore, sat on the riverbank and opened their picnic baskets. The

 feast had begun! It was just as he was finishing his last bite that Tip heard the sound of miaowing from somewhere nearby.

All the mice froze like statues – it was as if they had been turned to stone. The food fell from their paws as they realised with terror that it was Rowl – it had to be Rowl! It was the sound of their very worst enemy. They shook with fear, and some of the youngest mice started to cry.

'We're going to be eaten!' they wailed. 'Rowl will take us away and eat us!' But Tip whispered for them to be quiet because he was listening very carefully indeed.

'Something is wrong, I'm sure,' he said. 'I believe he's in trouble.'

Then Tip did a very brave thing, for it might have been that Rowl the cat was trying to trick them. Tip started off in the direction of the miaow he had heard – and went looking for Rowl! After a few minutes the mice by the riverbank heard his faint calling.

'I've found him! Come quickly!'

When the young mice arrived they couldn't believe their eyes. Rowl was lying stretched out on the ground with dirt on him from head to tail. One eye was bleeding and his paws were all sore and bruised. The dog that had chased him had left him frightened and badly hurt.

'Quick!' Tip cried. 'All of you run back to Haven Hill and fetch bandages and water. We must do all we can to help!'

Even though Rowl was their most feared and hated enemy the mice didn't wait to be told twice. They scattered before you could blink, and ran off to fetch little acorn shells of water and pawfuls of petals to clean Rowl's cuts. They tore up their picnic cloths to make into bandages and brought twigs to wipe away mud and old leaves from Rowl's fur.

Then, when they had done all they could, Tick and Pip were sent back as fast as they could run to find

Grevling the badger. In the meantime the mice made a sledge of twigs and grasses on which Rowl could be carried. When Grevling reached them they explained what had to be done and he pulled the sledge with the injured cat all the way back to the Hill.

For three days and nights the mice looked after Rowl. They brought him food when he was hungry and water when he was thirsty. Most of the time he just slept and

slept and slept. But one of the mice stayed with him all the time to keep watch over him, and there was even one mouse, called Kit, who sang songs by the cat's furry head.

On the morning of the fourth day Rowl opened his eyes and they shone with the first light of the sun.

'He's waking up!' shrieked Pip.

Tip came running to see. Rowl was trying to move his paws. He lifted his head, stretched, and struggled upwards. At first it was too much and he had to lie back down on the ground, but at last he stood up. All the mice had gathered in a semicircle to see him. They looked up at him, their old enemy, with great big eyes. They were tired after all they had done for Rowl, but they were happy too that he was well again at last.

'How can I thank you enough, my friends?' Rowl said to them all, and he bowed his big head towards them. 'I did not deserve your kindness and love after all I did to frighten and harm you. You had every right to leave me where I was to die. But even though I was your enemy you looked after me, you gave me everything you had until I was well again. I promise that for as long as I live I will be a friend to the mice, for I will never forget the kindness you have shown me. And if ever I can repay even a little of the love you have shown me then I will do so.'

(Reader's note: this story relates to the parable of The Good Samaritan, which can be found in Luke 10:25-37.)

# the Lamb

Angus hated the country. All the fields looked the same and it was always cold and miserable and muddy outside. His Aunt Jess made him fetch hay for her animals and go down to the bottom of the lane for milk early in the morning. He had to bring in whole bundles of logs from the shed for the fire. When he grew up he would live anywhere except a farm. He looked out of his bedroom window as the rain and sleet started falling once more over the fields. How he wished he was at home!

There were nine and a half days of the Easter holidays left before he went back to the town. That was if he counted the last morning. He couldn't wait to get away. Then he would be with his friends again! They could play football in the street and ride their bikes all round the old garage. There was never enough time in the city for all they wanted to do.

There was a knock at the door and his aunt came in.

'What about some cocoa?' she asked, tickling his feet.

He looked at the window and shook his head sadly.

'Not even with marshmallows?'

'I'm just going to go to sleep,' Angus said.

'All right, I'll be out at seven to check on the sheep. I'll waken you after I come in again and see if you'd like some tea. Sleep well, Angus.'

During the night the wind rose into a gale and Angus had strange dreams. His bedroom had become a cabin and the house was a ship, rocked about in the mighty blue waves of the Atlantic. He dreamed that he looked out of the window and the barn and the hen-house and the shed had all become strange islands, and the sheep white waves. He woke up in the morning feeling seasick.

But the next day it was just the same. He went down the track in the rain to fetch the milk. He took out hay to the animals and he brought in logs for the fire after tea. Every day was going to be the same until he went home. There were eight and a half days to go ...

During the night he was dreaming when he felt something tugging and tugging at his shoulder. He whimpered and tried to push it away. It was so snug and warm in bed ...

'Angus! Angus, wake up! There's something I want you to see!'

He struggled up in bed very grumpily indeed and rubbed his eyes. What on earth did his aunt want now?

Was there more work to be done on her stupid farm? It was the middle of the night! He looked at her extremely angrily and felt the chill of the room as he pulled back the covers.

She left the room and he got out of bed into the dark shadows of the room. He pulled on his warmest jumper and tied his shoes before thumping down the staircase to see what on earth she wanted. At least Coolin the sheepdog was there to meet him in the hall. Coolin was warm as a blanket and licked Angus' hand as he stroked her. Angus saw that the door was half open already and he realised that his aunt must have gone out before him. He sighed and followed her.

Outside it had been snowing. The world was all white and soft and there wasn't a breath of wind. The stars were shining up above like millions of diamonds. At least tomorrow he could go sledging, he thought. He saw a faint yellow light glowing from the  half-open doorway of the barn and he started over to it, the faithful Coolin padding behind.

The barn was warm. It smelled yellow and the air was full of straw dust that tickled his nose. He sneezed. When he opened his eyes again he saw his aunt crouched over in a far corner of the barn, holding the lantern in her right hand. There was a sheep in the corner, and beside it Angus saw the tiny bundle of a lamb.

'Come over and see,' his aunt whispered.

Angus' heart beat quickly as he went over, quiet as a mouse, to where the three of them were. The lamb had been born just a few minutes before and it was still all wet and shivering. But Angus thought it was the most beautiful thing he had ever seen in his life. He forgot all about feeling cold and tired, all about being annoyed and bored. This was magical.

Angus and his aunt sat there for ten minutes watching the newborn lamb and its mother.

'Are you glad you came after all?' his aunt whispered.

Angus nodded. 'Oh, yes! I'm sure I am!'

'It makes me think of Bethlehem,' she whispered. 'The day Jesus was born. Just as exciting as that, and with all the same sounds and scents as a barn like this. It must have been amazing.'

They looked at the lamb and its mother again, and Angus thought about the whole story of the coming of the shepherds and the kings to visit the special baby who had been born in a stable. Now it all seemed so real to him. He could imagine what it must have been like to be there all those centuries ago!

It was getting cold in the barn. In the end the two of them began shivering despite their woolly jumpers and coats.

'How about some cocoa then?' said Aunt Jess. 'With marshmallows?'

Angus nodded and grinned.

They went inside together and now Angus felt a warm glow in his tummy. Wait till he told his friends back home! There were lots of things he still missed from home in the town but somehow now they didn't seem to matter anymore. He would never forget seeing his first newborn lamb.

# the Old Man and the Lark

When you go as far west as it is possible to go, you will find an island. The wind blows there all year, summer and winter, autumn and spring. The hills are wild and rocky and the little golden beaches are hidden like secrets between the sharp rocks. In June the meadows are sweet with flowers and the nights are light blue and never dark.

Out on the last edges of the island shores there lived an old man called Sorley. All round the walls of his stone house hung the fiddles he had made, whose wood was dark as chestnuts and smooth as skin. They were made of the wood of ships that had been washed up on the shores, for not a single tree grew on the island itself.

Often Sorley was to be seen out in the storms and the rain, wandering among the shining rocks of the shore, searching for pieces of wood he could turn into fiddles. Then he would sit up all night, lovingly polishing and shaping the boards that had come from ships from Africa and Asia and America.

Sorley loved his island and knew every blade of grass and every birdsong. In springtime, he loved to find the nests of the moorland birds. He loved to call to the seals as they swam off the rocks when the waves were huge as horses and he loved to hear their singing. He loved to waken just before dawn and go out to the edge of the water as the light came pink and orange from the eastern skies.

Sorley knew every creature and bird on the island. When he walked over the moors he went quietly, never wanting to disturb all that was around him. He would watch the otter fishing in one of the deep river pools, diving and tumbling under the falls in silvery-gold. He knew where the robin built her nest in the bank each spring and he waited patiently for the day when the young birds learned to fly.

One summer day, Sorley crossed the moor when the light was white-blue and the buttercups crowded round his boots like a golden sea. He heard the breeze sighing and whispering in the buttercup stems like hundreds of tiny voices. He looked out over the sea at scattering of islands that shone like strange dark jewels in the light.

All of a sudden he looked up into the sky and saw a sparrowhawk fluttering high above, hunting. Sorley stopped walking and looked about him, wondering what the hawk had spied. All about him the golden the buttercups swayed and whispered in the wind.

Then he felt the tiniest touch on his left boot. The old man looked down. There on the middle of his foot was a lark. Its tiny breast was beating fiercely. It looked up at Sorley with its bright shining beads of eyes as if it was asking him to protect it, to keep it safe from the terrible danger of the sparrowhawk.

Very gently, Sorley knelt down among the buttercups and kept watch over the tiny lark that clung to his boot. The lark was no bigger than your clenched fist. He did not move, minute after minute, but kept crouching there with his hands folded on his knee, guarding the bird whose song he knew and loved so much.

And the lark stayed there safe on the old man's boot until the sparrowhawk had given up its hunt and flown away, and the dark shadow was gone at last.

Only then did the lark look up once more at Sorley as if in thanks and flew up from the old man's boot into the sky. Sorley gazed into the blue sky as the little lark rose higher and higher, twirling beautiful symphonies of song in joy and gratitude.

And that night in the quiet of his house on the rocks, as the stars glittered like the edges of waves in the great sea of the sky, Sorley played on his fiddle the notes of the song the lark had sung for him after it was saved from the sparrowhawk. It was the most beautiful gift he had ever been given.

# the Nest

The spring had come at last. There was blossom on the trees and the days were growing longer and longer. All winter Archie had been used to coming home from school as it was beginning to get dark. He hated that – it meant that he and his best friends never went outside at all and had to sit for hours doing maths and French.

Now at four o'clock the sun was still up in the sky and the days of rain were over. With every week that passed the summer holidays were coming that bit closer.

One Thursday afternoon it was just perfect. There wasn't a cloud in the sky as Archie ran out of school as fast as he could with George and Sam.

'Meet you in ten minutes at the back of the shop!' he shouted. That was where they always gathered to decide what they most wanted to do on any particular day. Usually they went into the shop first for a packet of sweets and stood outside in a ring, talking and sharing all they'd bought.

'I'll be back for tea!' Archie shouted after he'd run into the porch and flung his bag across the hall. 'Can't stop, George and Sam are waiting …'

He caught a glimpse of his mother in the hall. She was about to say something but he had already slammed the door behind him before she had time to think. It was just about the same as any other day. She picked up the washing with a sigh and went outside. At least it was a perfect afternoon for drying clothes.

Sam and Archie nearly crashed into each other as they came running round the back of the shop. Archie nearly choked on a bit of chocolate, trying to eat it far too fast. They could see George hurrying up the hill and they waved for him to hurry.

'Sorry,' he said, almost out of breath. 'I had to do some dishes.'

'Shall we go down to the river?' Sam asked. 'We could finish the den.'

'There's too many people there,' said George, screwing up his face. 'It's better on a Saturday, after everyone's gone home.'

They thought about it as they chewed on caramels.

'What about the wood?' Archie suggested.

The other two looked at him for a moment, not saying anything. They knew they weren't supposed to go there on their own. But it was a perfect idea, and there would be just enough time if they set off right then.

'I'm not sure …' Sam was worried. He knew what sort of row he'd get.

'Oh, come on!' George said. 'They don't have to find out. It'd be ace!'

That was two against one and Sam had to agree. The last thing he wanted them to think was that he was too scared. They ran along the footpath at the back of the town and turned then behind the school and the church onto another path that curled and twisted right to the edge of the wood. It looked so deep and dark – there wasn't so much as the song of one bird coming from the trees.

It had been Archie's idea and Archie led the way. After a bit the path seemed to disappear altogether and the three boys had to push branches out of the way and creep along, their backs almost bent double. Even Archie felt strange and wondered for a moment if it had been a good idea after all. But there was no way he could turn back now – the others would laugh at him for sure.

Then, all of a sudden, they broke out into a clearing. They stood there together, getting their breath back and brushing off the pine needles and twigs from their uniforms. Suddenly, a bird with blue on its wings flew out of a tree.

'That was a jay!' Sam hissed, pointing excitedly. 'I bet you anything it has a nest up there!'

George grabbed Archie's arm. 'You're the best at climbing,' he said. 'Why not go up and get the eggs? Go on Archie! We could take them into school tomorrow – it would be magic!'

For a second Archie wasn't sure. For one thing he was going to get even more dirty than he already was. But all the same …

'All right, take my blazer. Tell me if you hear anybody coming.'

He swung himself up into the first branches. He had to fight with them to see what he was doing, to have an idea of where to put his feet next. He was scared he would get a branch in the eye. Then he found the next hold, and the next. Bit by bit he swung himself higher until he glanced back and saw Sam and George a long way below him. They were telling him what to do next, shouting encouragement as twigs stuck in his shirt and he battled to see what on earth he was doing.

Then, all at once, he was there, looking in on a nest with four blue eggs the size of small plums. He opened his mouth in surprise and wonder – they were so beautiful.

'What is it, Archie? What have you found?' George shouted.

But Archie couldn't say a word. This was one of the most beautiful things he had ever seen in his life. He remembered what his aunt had told him, about God making the world and everything that was in it. He hadn't really thought about it until now. But those eggs were so beautiful, and each one of them contained a tiny life, a bird that would grow and learn to fly just like the other jays. Archie moved away very gently so as not to disturb the eggs. He started climbing down as George and Sam kept calling to ask what the matter was.

'Come on, we're going home,' he said. The eggs mustn't be allowed to get cold. Going into the wood had been his idea and it was his decision to go back home. He would tell his friends about the nest on the way. He was glad he'd left the eggs. He knew it was the right thing to do.

# the Island

It was late in June and Jamie's parents had found a wooden cottage on an island where they were going to stay three whole weeks. Jamie counted the days on the calendar – he longed for the last day of school to be over.

Finally the holidays arrived. They left the city very early on a Saturday morning and drove all night. Jamie slept on the back seat of the car and sometimes he woke up and thought of the island that was getting closer every minute. It gave him a feeling like butterflies in his tummy.

At last they came to a place where they went on board a ferry with red funnels. For four hours they sailed further and further out into the ocean until they couldn't see land at all. Then, out of the distance, the island appeared and it began to grow bigger and clearer all the time.

'Can you see our cottage?' Jamie's dad asked, and he put a pair of binoculars round Jamie's neck.

Jamie searched and searched, and at last he found a little brown speck that might have been their wooden cottage.

And it was. When they got there Jamie took off his shoes and walked about the house in his bare feet. Everything smelled of sand and wood. When he went to bed that night he could hear the seabirds calling and calling – it was as if they were crying his name with their high-pitched voices, 'Ja-mie! Ja-mie!'

Every day there were new adventures to be had. He went swimming with his mum and dad in the blue-green water and the three of them explored a cave together. They watched an otter playing in the shallow water near their beach and one evening Jamie was lucky enough to find a whole sea urchin on the sand.

The days passed quick as you could blink and, one evening, Jamie's dad reminded him he'd have to pack. They were going to leave for home the following day. There was sand in everything Jamie had – his books, his socks and even his glasses. It took him a long time to pack and he didn't feel like sleeping at all.

The following morning he woke up very early indeed, long before it was properly light. He dressed quickly and went over to the window. There was just enough light to see by – it was going to be the most beautiful day.

Suddenly Jamie decided he was going to run down to their beach – the one that was closest to the house. He tiptoed along the wooden corridor so he wouldn't waken his mum and dad and very carefully turned the handle of the outer wooden door. He ran to the bottom of the garden, opened the little gate and was down on the shore in no time at all.

There wasn't another soul in the world to be seen. Jamie might have been the only person alive. He listened to the silky waves as they folded over the white shell sand, and he watched the sun as it began to break through the dark skies into dawn. He had never before felt quite so happy and peaceful – he wanted it to last for always. He didn't want to go home at all – he wished they could stay for ever and ever. Then he noticed a little pink cowrie shell at his feet. It was the only thing on the whole beach and he picked it up carefully from the sand – put it safely at the very bottom of his pocket.

Then everything seemed to happen very fast. Before he'd thought about it he'd had his breakfast and the car was packed. They drove on to the ferry and already the island was growing small and dim. They were back on the straight main road driving with all the busy traffic towards the city and home. Everything now seemed to be grey – all the wonderful blues and greens and golds of the island had disappeared in no time at all.

'School tomorrow,' his mum reminded him gently before he went upstairs to bed that evening. 'Better make sure your bag's ready.'

When he got to bed in the end Jamie's heart felt heavy as lead. He listened to the cars roaring past in the darkness and he thought what it would be like on the island – just the calling and crying of the birds and the rippling sound of the waves falling one after another on to the great white beaches. Jamie felt his eyes filling with tears and he cried and he cried and he cried. At last he heard his mum coming into the room and kneeling at his bedside.

'What is it?' she asked gently and put her hand through his hair. 'Is it because the holiday's over?'

Jamie nodded. 'I miss the island and I'm frightened of school and I was so happy!' He couldn't see for the hot tears in his eyes.

'I know, Jamie,' his mum said understandingly, and she sat beside him on the bed. 'Sit up for a moment and listen to me.'

He sniffed and wiped his eyes and sat up. His mum reached over to Jamie's bedside table and picked up the little cowrie shell he'd found on the beach early that morning. She smiled and held it against his ear.

'Can you hear anything?' she whispered. 'Listen carefully!'

He held his breath and listened. 'I think so. I think I can hear the sea.'

His mum nodded and smiled to him. 'The island will always be with you, if you let it. You've got to keep it safe, deep inside your heart. Just like God. He'll always be with you, if you let him, helping you through all the bad days at school and keeping you close to him. D'you see?'

Jamie nodded. He did see.

'Go to sleep, then. Dream about the island – we'll go back there again, I promise you!'

And he did.

# Lia's New Friend

It was July and the days were as they should be in the middle of summer. The sun didn't disappear from the sky until ten o'clock at night, and it was so warm that when you went along the stone path at the back of the house in bare feet your toes felt as if they were burning. Down at the river the children played and laughed until late in the evening. At nine o'clock the last of them went slowly home, towels dangling from their hands.

But Lia didn't join them. Two months ago she had come with her mum and dad to Scotland from Helsinki in Finland. Everything was different, everything was horrid. How she missed all the lakes in Finland and the wonderful pine forest at the back of the house! In a few weeks' time the holidays would be over and she would have to begin school here. How she was dreading it!

'Why don't you go and swim with the others?' her mother asked. 'I'm sure they'd be friendly to you. Give it a try!'

But Lia shook her head. Instead she looked at pictures of her granny back in Helsinki and tears stung her eyes. She missed her so badly it hurt.

Her dad came and said hat he would go with her to the river if she wanted, but she told him she had a sore foot. He sighed and went away and the house was big and silent. There wasn't an attic to play in like at home in Finland. The bedroom she had now looked out on a boring old street and a sweet shop. At night it wasn't easy to get to sleep because of the noise of the traffic. The sunlight filled her room like yellow blossom and for a minute she thought longingly of the river. She loved swimming more than anything...

At nine o'clock that evening she was out in the garden playing when she heard the others coming back from the river. They were laughing and shouting, and she hid behind a firtree so they wouldn't see her. She felt shy. They were throwing things at a terrier puppy that had followed them.

'Ya! Get away! Stupid dog!'

The terrier hid behind a tree stump and lay down, whimpering. One by one the children went on along the path towards the village, laughing and chatting as they ran. Lia came out from behind the tree and made sure she was alone. She went forward to the gate and opened it, went a little closer to the terrier. He watched her with frightened golden eyes, still whimpering. She bent down.

'Come on,' she whispered. 'I won't do anything to hurt you.'

Very slowly the little dog came towards her. Lia didn't move a muscle, terrified in case she might frighten him and scare him away. All the time she whispered in Finnish, her hand held out in kindness.

Suddenly she realised that the dog and she were not so different after all. Here she was, a stranger from Finland whom nobody spoke to or understood. The terrier was just the same. He was on his own and no one wanted him around. That made Lia want to make friends with him all the more.

'Come on, puppy,' she whispered. 'I'll look after you, I promise!'

At last the terrier came so close that there was just a hair's breadth between her hand and the top of his head. At the very last moment she thought he might lose confidence and turn to run away, but instead he let her stroke the furry bit above his eyes. He sat down and lay with his head between his paws, watching her all the time. But his eyes weren't nearly as frightened as they had been before.

Suddenly Lia turned round and saw her dad standing watching her. He was smiling and shaking his head.

'Please can I keep him, dad?' she begged. 'He's so beautiful, and no one else wants him. He was just here in the wood all on his own!'

'Let's see then,' her dad said gently. 'But maybe somebody's missing him. We'll have to be sure he doesn't have a home somewhere else.'

For three days Lia waited, hardly able to breathe because she was so afraid somebody might come to ask for Scamp back. But nobody came, and her dad said that Scamp could be hers.

The following Saturday it was so hot that she couldn't resist going down to the river to swim. Scamp came along with her, faithfully trotting at her heels and sniffing for rabbits. She heard the laughter and shouts of the others and at first she was afraid. She felt her heart pounding in her chest. But she felt braver with Scamp. Everyone did look at her when she first arrived. They were curious about where she came from and about the strange language she spoke. But then a girl called Esther showed her the best pool for swimming and Lia dived in. The others watched her diving and twisting in the water. None of them could swim like that.

When Lia got out with them later she introduced Scamp to them. He had been sitting patiently among the hot stones on the shore, watching his beloved mistress all the time. Now no one was nasty to Scamp at all; they patted him and ruffled his ears.

Lia went home with all the others that evening. She was dusty and tired but she felt very happy all the same. Her mum and dad were there to meet her at the garden gate. Last of all Scamp came in too, and shook the river water from his back.

Lia smiled. She knew God had looked after her even though she had often doubted that he would. The days ahead wouldn't be so easy, but she knew now without any doubt that she would be kept safe.

# the Fox's tale

Young Fergal of Haven Hill was a cub no longer. He was growing into a strong fox, eager to explore the world. He knew every corner of the wood and had had plenty of adventures there. He loved Haven Hill very much but he longed to know what lay further over in the next valley. In the evening he could see the last rays of the sun shining on the fields and the trees there, and it made him feel excited and restless. Who lived there? Where did the paths lead? How long would it take to get there?

Most of all, Fergal wanted to know if the city lay in that direction. He had overheard two of the badgers talking about the city one evening and it had made him feel all strange and excited. There were lights there that never went out, and all sorts of strange creatures that lived in dens and burrows. Now Haven Hill seemed dull to Fergal. The nights were long and, during the day, the only creatures he ever saw were the ones he had always known. If only he could leave to find the city! But he knew that his mother and father would tell him he was still too young, that it wasn't safe for a fox of his age to leave home on his own.

One summer day Fergal was lying among the brambles watching a butterfly flopping lazily among  the flowers. His mother and father were busy tidying the den and the young fox was glad to be on his own. He was dreaming of the adventures he would have when he could get away from Haven Hill at last.

'Hello, young fox, do you know where Greenwell is from here?'

Fergal jumped up. 'Greenwell's just at the bottom of the hill.'

The other fox had black tips to his bushy ears and a white tip to his tail.

'My name's Freddy,' he said. 'I'm just passing through. On my way back to the city.'

'The city?' Fergal exclaimed, unable to believe his ears. 'Are you really? Please, Freddy, would I be able to come with you? I'm longing for adventure!'

Freddy smiled. 'Well, I don't know. You'd better ask your family.'

Fergal was off before you could say foxglove. 'Mother, I've just met the most amazing fox and he's said he'll let me go with him to the city. I'm tired of Haven Hill and I've said that I want to go with him.'

Fergal's mother looked sadly at her beloved cub. 'All right then, if you've made up your mind, Fergal, then you will have to go. We will miss you very much, you know. Be careful and remember we are always here for you when you need us.'

Fergal hardly looked at either his mother or father to say goodbye. He bounded off, frightened that perhaps Freddy had left for the city without him. But there he was, waiting.

'I'm ready!' cried Fergal with excitement, his heart beating like a drum. 'Let's go!' They ran down past Greenwell Farm and on to the sandy track.

At last, after going through a deep wood, they came out on to the railway line. Freddy told Fergal that if they followed the track it would take them all the way to the city. Fergal could hardly believe his ears. Soon he would be there at last! What adventures lay before him!

They reached the city at nightfall. Fergal couldn't believe all the noise around him and the rushing of feet. There were so many lights and strange buildings. It was all so exciting! At last they reached the safety of Freddy's den, hidden deep under a busy road.

'Now we can go and raid some bins for dinner!' Freddy said. 'Come on, young fox, you've got a lot to learn!' How different it was from eating at home on Haven Hill! There was always enough there. In the city they had to knock over rubbish bins and pick out old chicken bones and bags of smelly leftovers. One old woman came rushing from her house with a broom to chase the foxes away.

The following day, Freddy told Fergal he had to visit another fox on the far side of the city. Fergal stayed on his own in the dark den. It wasn't warm and cosy like at home on Haven Hill. Outside it was stormy and the young fox could hear the distant grumbling of thunder and the hammering of rain. He tried to sleep but he was kept awake by the endless roaring of the traffic. He was cold and wet and hungry.

'Why did I ever come here?' he thought. 'I have everything I need at home. How could I have been so foolish as to run away to this terrible place?' He decided there and then that he would go home that very night. He hardly knew the way but he couldn't bear another day in that place in the city he had dreamed so long of finding.

After a long time he found the railway line and started along it. By early morning he realised he had come to the wood Freddy and he had crossed and he made his way back along the track that led to Greenwell Farm. His paws were so sore he could hardly walk.

There on the edge of Haven Hill he saw to his amazement his father watching and waiting for him. It looked almost as if he had been there since the afternoon Freddy took him away to the city. For the first time the young fox realised how much he cared about home and Haven Hill – how could he ever have imagined he might leave forever?

'Please forgive me for running away,' the young fox said. 'I know I was foolish and selfish.'

'Of course you are forgiven, Fergal,' his father said. 'No matter how far away you may go from us, we will always be there for you if you choose to come home. That is what the love of a father and mother is like. Never forget that.'

(Reader's note: this story relates to the parable of The Prodigal Son, which can be found in Luke 15:11–32.)

# the Acorn

andy was bored. It was a Saturday afternoon and there was nothing to do. Her friends were all away doing this and that with their families and she seemed to be the only person left in the village for the weekend. It was what her mother called a nothing day.

The mist was hanging in the trees and there wasn't the slightest sound of the wind. Everything was dead still and the river flowed by like a wolf. It wasn't really light and it wasn't really dark. It was a nothing day at the very beginning of autumn and Sandy was bored.

'Why don't you go cycling?' her dad asked. Sandy shook her head. She had a flat tyre.

'Why don't you go into town?' Sandy looked sad. Because she had no money.

Her father thought for a minute. She could tell he was thinking. He always looked up at the window and stared without blinking when he was trying hard to think.

'I know,' he said suddenly, so sharply that he made
her jump. 'Go and get your gumboots and come with
me. On you go – I promise you'll be glad you did.'

Very reluctantly, Sandy went and got her boots and
coat. In a way she wished she had said yes to one of
his earlier ideas. Probably now he was going to ask her
to do some weeding in the back garden or to rake up
the leaves on the lawn. But it was too late now so she
would just have to grin and bear it.

When she met her dad in the hall she found he
was wearing his coat too, and carrying a rather silly
umbrella. She hoped that wherever they were going
they wouldn't meet too many people.

'All right then,' he said, 'let's go. We're off to the
wood.'

Sandy still didn't really understand why. Sometimes her dad went on long walks by himself and he certainly walked through the wood on his way. But it was strange that that was where he wanted to go now. Still, there was no point in arguing.

They got to the wood in the end. The path they took was very muddy after all the long days and nights of early autumn rain. The mist was everywhere – just a little bit in front of them all the time – and when Sandy breathed it was like swallowing cotton wool.

All the same, they got to the wood in the end. They went into one of the clearings and stopped. The only sounds were of the river close by and the woodpigeons' voices in the branches overhead.

'Right, I want you to find a handful of acorns,' Sandy's dad said to her. She wondered if he had been out in the sun too long in the summer. What on earth was he on about? All the same, she began searching for acorns among the leaves under the great trees. It took her a long time, but at last she had gathered a whole handful. Some of the acorns she found were a bit cracked and battered, but they were whole. Her father had found a great handful too.

'All right, we can go home now,' he said.

Sandy decided he had definitely gone completely and utterly off his head. She looked at him in a very worried way and then followed him as he began marching back along the muddy path. This was the strangest walk she could remember in her whole life.

But when they got home they didn't go inside. At the back of the house she saw that her dad had prepared a whole collection of little plant pots, all neatly filled with soil. He took an acorn from Sandy's hand and pushed it down into the pot. Together they did that with each of the acorns they had found.

Sandy forgot all about the walk with her dad and the acorns until the spring came back once more and she looked again at the row of brown plant pots in the back garden. In some of them now were strong little green shoots that were stretching up above the rims of the pots. They were tiny trees.

'D'you know why I brought those acorns home?' her dad asked.

Sandy shook her head. She still didn't really understand what the walk on that nothing day in autumn had been all about.

'Well, God gave us this wonderful earth to live in, but he also made us its stewards. That means that he made us responsible for all the beauty around us. We have to look after it and care for it in the very best way we can. That shows God that we care about him too. Just think of all the acorns there are lying about in the forest – hundreds and hundreds of them. Some of them get crushed by our boots, others get eaten, and most of them die just where they fall. But inside every acorn is a tree waiting to happen – a whole oak tree! We won't ever see it full-grown, but the people who come after us will! Planting an acorn is a way of saying thank you to God for all the wonder of the world. It's a way of telling him that we understand how precious it is and that we want to be his stewards.'

Now at last Sandy understood what the acorns had been for. She realised suddenly that it was possible after all for one small person on the planet to make a difference by caring for a wonderful earth. And if everybody carried home a pocketful of acorns to plant tiny new oak trees, then what a difference it would make to the world – and what a way of saying thank you to God!

# the Robin

Esther's dad always took her to the park on a Saturday in her wheelchair. Often the others from school would come down to play on the swings and the chute, and they would run over to Esther with sherbet and lollies. Esther's dad would go off birdwatching in the nearby woods and leave Esther there with the others, knowing she would be happy to talk and laugh with them until lunch-time.

It was October and on this particular Saturday Esther had woken up very early in the morning, even though it was so dark. There was something funny about the room and the whole house, she was sure of it. It made her think of a time when she was very young indeed, but she couldn't quite remember what it was that had happened. The quiet was so huge, and outside the rush of traffic didn't begin at six o'clock as usual. That was very strange. What on earth was it? She lay half-asleep for the next hour and a half, just listening and wondering, until at last her dad knocked on the door and came in.

She looked at him and laughed. Now she understood. He was covered in big wet snowflakes! It must have snowed through the night.

'Can we go to the park? Please, Dad! They'll all be there for the snow!'

Esther and her dad had breakfast together and Esther kept looking outside to make sure the snow was still there. She was half afraid it might suddenly vanish when her back was turned.

Her dad helped her dress, and then he packed the wheelchair tight with a good coat so she wouldn't freeze. Last of all he put on a bright padded jacket and a tall woolly hat the colour of a pillar box. Esther groaned.

'Please, Dad, no. You look like a garden gnome! Not that hat!'

In the end she let him wear a rather old battered cap because he said that otherwise his bald head would get cold. Last of all he picked up his binoculars in the hall and put them round his neck. They were ready to go.

Outside, the town was in chaos. Cars were spinning as they tried to get up hills and a bus was stuck in the middle of the High Street. Esther's dad had to keep a strong hold on her chair to make sure it didn't speed up and run all the way to the park on its own!

Nobody had expected snow in October – it had taken them all by surprise. Everyone was talking about the weather – the old ladies in the post office and the men outside the bank. You could tell from their faces what they were talking about!

The only people who were happy were the children. They threw snowballs at the statues outside the school and they hit the postman on the back of the neck with a snowball as he was putting letters into the box at the Town Hall. He was very angry indeed and chased them for a bit, his cheeks burning. But they ran off laughing and disappeared behind the library. There was no point trying to catch them and he soon gave up.

At last Esther and her dad got to the park. It was like a fairyland with the snow on the lamp-posts and the benches. Everything was magical and the snow was still falling, big as cats' paws. Then Esther saw her friends beside the bowling green, which was white instead of green, and they came running to meet her, calling her name as they went.

'Hi, Esther, how're you doing?'

'Hello, Mr Ryan. Are you off birdwatching?'

'D'you want some chocolate, Esther? You can have a drink from the flask later on if you want.'

She felt really happy that her friends were there. It wouldn't be the same without them. But then Tommy discovered that there was ice on the hill and he called to them to come and help him build a slide. Suddenly they were all gone. They were all laughing and shrieking with joy as they threw themselves down the steep hill towards the bowling green. Esther's dad had left a moment or two before to go off to the wood to look for birds and Esther was completely alone. She wished more than ever before that she could walk and run like all the others, that she wasn't stuck in her wretched wheelchair! Why did life have to be so unfair? Why should everything be so much harder for her than for everyone else? Her friends just forgot about her as soon as their backs were turned. Not even one of them bothered to sit and talk to her.

She felt tears springing to the backs of her eyes, she felt them misting with a mixture of sadness and anger. She knew that God loved her but why then was it sometimes so hard to feel it?

Suddenly Esther saw a robin landing on a lamp-post near her. It looked at her with its head on one side, its chest rising and falling as it breathed.

'Hello, robin,' she whispered, and now she hoped that none of her friends would come back too suddenly and frighten the bird. Her heart beat with excitement. She put her hand deep into her jacket pocket and found to her delight part of a biscuit that had broken there and been forgotten days before. She held the crumbs out on the palm of her hand.

'Come on, robin, don't be afraid,' she said, and she scattered some of the crumbs on the snow in front of her wheelchair.

The robin saw the crumbs and flew down to the ground. But when he was finished he looked up at Esther, let out a little jewel of sound, and flew up on to her open palm. Without fear he ate the last crumbs from her fingers. This was better than sledging, she thought, or building a slide. She remembered again that God loved her, that he cared for her as a special person, just as she was. And she felt good and warm inside.

# the Shoemaker

'I don't want to go and get my stupid shoes! Tom and I were going to get conkers up in the wood!'

Simon was furious. Why should he go down town to get his mended shoes just after coming back from school? By the time he had done that it was bound to be dark and he could forget going to get conkers until the weekend. Jason and Andrew would be sure to find all the best ones now.

But his mum wasn't going to give in. He sighed very heavily when he went through the

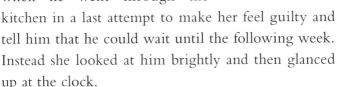

kitchen in a last attempt to make her feel guilty and tell him that he could wait until the following week. Instead she looked at him brightly and then glanced up at the clock.

'On you go. You'll be back in good time if you go for them now. The shop shuts at five so you'd better get going.'

He sighed again and trailed out into the hall. His sister Joanna gave him the most sickly smile as she passed him and he would have loved to kick her. But then he would be grounded all weekend and there would be no going for conkers at all. It wasn't worth it. He dragged his jacket from its hook and banged the door really loudly behind him.

It wasn't raining outside but a very thin drizzle was falling, the kind that seemed to sink right into your bones. The town was almost completely empty and everything was horrible and grey. He felt the same horrible grey colour inside, as if it was drizzling somewhere there too. He walked along the river-bank for a few minutes and decided that the only things in the world that were happy were the ducks. That made him feel even madder and more drizzly than before.

At ten to five Simon reached the shoemaker's. He had hoped that he might get there just a minute or two too late so that he could trail home again completely wet and make his mum feel guilty because she had sent him all that way for nothing. But the shoemaker's was still open and there was nothing for it but for Simon to go on in.

'Hello, Mr Norris,' Simon said, 'I've come to pick up my shoes.'

Mr Norris was very old and very slow. He nodded to Simon and wiped his hands on his dirty apron and turned round to disappear upstairs into his workshop.

Simon looked about him. It was strange in there, almost like another world. It was as if he had fallen down a strange hole and come out somewhere else entirely. All around the walls were very old posters for shoes and shoe polish. Many of them were faded and torn, and the writing on them was strange and difficult to read.

The whole place smelled brown. The air was brown and the floor was brown and the walls were brown. It wasn't like a modern shop at all, with bright lights and music and lots of big windows. This was the kind of shop Simon imagined his grandpa might have remembered.

He thought how important shoemakers must have been once upon a time. Nowadays hardly anyone made shoes by hand – machines did everything. But when his grandpa was a boy, shoemakers must have been very busy! Everybody needed to get to places, they all had important journeys to make, and so they all had to have shoes for their feet.

Simon heard Mr Norris coming slowly downstairs. He gasped as he saw his old shoes – they were so beautifully polished! They were like new! He remembered kicking stones with them and going through mud and getting them caught in barbed wire fences. They had been scratched and torn and grey when he handed them in and now they were gleaming – just like brand new conkers that have fallen out of their shells!

'Thank you!' he gasped with amazement and took them proudly from the old man's hands. 'They're magic!'

The old man laughed but somehow that too was almost like magic. The shine from the mended shoes seemed to fill the whole shop and as Simon turned

them in his hands he could see the reflection of his own smile. He paid for the shoes and thanked the old man again before going out of the shop into the drizzly afternoon.

Simon didn't even want to get drizzle on his shoes – he didn't want anything at all to spoil them.

Then he remembered all of a sudden just how he had been when he left the house earlier on. He felt ashamed that he had been so angry with his mother and shouted at her. There had been no real need for him to bang the door as he had done. He looked again at his shoes. In a way maybe God and the shoemaker had something in common. Every day Simon shouted and said things he shouldn't have and felt angry with his sister. Every night in his prayer he said sorry to God for it all and he really felt that God heard his prayer! It was like waking up in the morning to find a brand new pair of shoes beside the bed! All the scuffs and the scratches were gone – everything was beautiful again.

When Simon reached home he went inside very quietly and laid his shoes down in the hall without a sound. There was his mum at the top of the stairs. She looked up and smiled when she saw him.

'I'm sorry, mum' he said softly. 'I'll try not to shout like that again.'

He was even quite nice to his sister Joanna that evening.

# the Present

I t was Helen's birthday. She woke up when it was still dark and she listened. She could hear the rain singing and dancing on the roofs of the houses round about. Her heart sank. It was school today – a normal Thursday with double maths and games. They would have to play hockey in the rain.

She got up grumpily and dragged on her clothes. She opened her curtains and saw the rain falling like rods of iron on to the pavements and the houses in the street. The only colour in the world was grey. Why was her birthday in November? Why couldn't she have been born in May like her best friend Sarah? It wasn't fair.

Helen clumped heavily downstairs and tried her best to smile as she sat down with her mum and dad at the breakfast table. There was a small parcel waiting on her plate, beautifully wrapped with paper that was covered in pictures of horses.

'I'm afraid it's only a small present this birthday, Helen,' said her mum. 'Because your dad lost his job last month things aren't so easy for us as they were. But we'll try to make it a special day all the same.'

Helen smiled again, but she still didn't feel like it. She carefully unwrapped the little box to find a necklace inside with a golden pony on it. She thanked her parents many times for their kindness and put it on at once. Then she ate her breakfast at top speed and ran out to get her coat and boots so as not to be late for school.

'I'm afraid I can't give you a lift,' her dad said sadly. 'There's something wrong with the car and I won't be able to get it fixed until the beginning of next month. Will you be all right?'

'I'll probably meet Sarah on the way,' Helen said. 'I'll be fine ...'

She picked up her schoolbag and closed the front door behind her. But she didn't feel fine at all – she felt absolutely rotten. She had never felt so miserable in all her life. It was as if there was a dark lump in her stomach. She could feel the golden pony against her throat. Why couldn't it have been a real pony, like the ones that Jane and Liz had?

Why couldn't she get a proper present – one she could boast about in school? Everyone would laugh at the gold pony – it wasn't even real gold. Susan Smith would laugh especially – she always knew how to make Helen feel really stupid and embarrassed.

Helen met Sarah on the way to school after all and that cheered her up a bit. But in double maths Mrs Gracie shouted at her for getting something wrong when she wasn't concentrating and Susan Smith smirked at her triumphantly. In break, when all the girls were out in the playground, someone asked her what her parents had given her for her birthday.

'There wasn't time for them to give me my present before school,' she answered quickly, looking away. She felt her cheeks burning with shame and guilt. The little gold pony seemed heavy as lead about her neck.

'I thought they were giving you a new pair of glasses,' Susan Smith said loudly, 'so you could see the ball better in hockey.'

Everyone except Sarah laughed and drifted away to play games. It was still raining and Helen felt as if the cold and the wet had gone right into her heart. She wanted to cry but she knew that was the one thing she mustn't do. She couldn't wait for the day to be over – then she could go home and be on her own. That was all she wanted.

Games seemed to last for ever. At least the rain had stopped but the playing fields were soaking wet and she was covered with muddy splashes ten minutes after the match started. The whole way through she kept thinking it was so unfair that people couldn't choose when their birthdays were and how they wanted to celebrate them.

In the evening her mum made her favourite dinner and they sat together to watch a film. Helen knew how hard they were trying to make it a really special day for her, but she knew too that they could see she was down. In the end she said she was tired and wanted to go to bed early. She trailed upstairs and fell asleep.

But during the night she had a very strange dream. It was about a man she'd heard of who'd gone to a country called Romania to help the people there because they were so poor. In her mind she saw the man bending down to give a present of a little teddy bear to a girl of her own age. The girl had never had a present in all her life. The little teddy bear was very ordinary – it wasn't all that special or expensive. But to the girl it meant the world. In the dream Helen saw her carrying it with her everywhere she went.

When Helen woke up the next morning the rain had stopped. She lay thinking about the dream and, when it was time to get up, she ran downstairs as fast as she could. Her mum and dad were already sitting at the breakfast table as she came in. She went to each of them and gave them the biggest hug she could. She knew that God had given her so much to be thankful for – a wonderful home and family.

'What did we do to deserve this?' her dad said, smiling.

'I just wanted to tell you that I love you and that I'm glad I have you,' said Helen.

# Amy's Christmas

my was counting the days until Christmas. She had put the advent calendar up on the mantelpiece and every morning when she came downstairs she would carefully open another window. There was an angel blowing a trumpet and a lamb in a stable and a giant star with red and blue flames around it in the night sky.

Amy had helped her mother to make the house ready for Christmas. They had gone out together to the wood to cut giant bits of holly from the trees with plenty of red berries. The wood was secret and dark, with frost in the branches and on the path

where they walked. The holly was all shiny and glassy, and difficult to carry because each piece was prickly. When they came home they put the holly in the windows, beside the lamps and around the Christmas cards.

Amy had helped her father to put up the Christmas tree and decorate it with tinsel and balls, and at the very top they had put the shining star of Bethlehem.

Then finally her dad wrapped the Christmas lights around the branches and turned them on. The room was beautiful but still Amy felt a little bleak, as if something were not quite right, as if something were missing ...

She went carol singing through the village and enjoyed all the laughter, the song, and the presents they were given. She watched the first snow falling early one morning and she went out to feed a robin, holding crumbs in the palm of her hand so that the little bird might come down and eat from it. There were plenty of exciting things to eat, places to go and things to do, but always there was something missing and she could not work out what it was.

Christmas Eve came at last and the fire was lit. Amy's mother lit candles too and put them on the mantelpiece and in the hall. The snow was thick outside and there was ice on the window-sills. Amy looked out and saw the lights of the farms far up in the hills and thought how everyone there would be looking forward to Christmas just as much as she was.

Her stocking was ready waiting beside her bed to be filled with presents. Her mother had said that she could wait up until her father came home from work before she went to bed.

At eight o'clock there was a noise at the door and she ran to meet her dad. But to her great surprise he was not alone. With him was a man dressed in the oldest clothes, with his hair all bedraggled and messy. He was very thin and frightened-looking, and Amy's father was leading him by the arm.

'This is Michael,' he said. 'Michael has nowhere to go this Christmas. He doesn't have a home or any friends and I said that he could come and spend Christmas with us.'

Amy didn't know what to say. She felt very shy as she looked at the stranger. She wasn't sure if she wanted to share her home with someone else at Christmas. But at once her mother went running to find something warm for Michael to drink and a thick jumper for him to wear. He looked cold and hungry and his hands were all red and swollen.

At first Amy didn't know what to talk to Michael about, but then she told him how she had helped her father to put up the Christmas tree and decorate the house, and which parts she had done all by herself. She told him about what presents she hoped might be waiting for her in the morning and about the igloo she wanted to build with her friends if there was enough snow. And after Michael had eaten something and was warm from sitting closer to the fire, he smiled and nodded and laughed happily with Amy.

In the end it was bedtime and she said goodnight to everyone, including Michael. In the morning she found her stocking and opened all the presents she had been given. She had so many that it was wonderfully exciting. Then she remembered Michael. She didn't have any present for him. What would he like? She looked among her presents and she found the one she liked best – a little glass ball with a house inside and lots of woolly snowflakes. When you took the globe and shook it, all the snowflakes swirled about and landed at last on the roof and the trees and the ground outside the little house. She wanted very much to keep it for herself. It was one of the loveliest presents she had ever had. But she wanted to give it to Michael, because he had nothing at all.

So that Christmas Day when all the presents were being given out she went over and gave the globe with the snowstorm to Michael. She could see that he was very, very pleased and he thanked her many times. Together they laughed as he shook the globe and the little snowflakes rose up into the air time after time to swirl back down once again.

When Amy went to bed that night, she lay in the darkness thinking. She remembered how she had felt before Christmas came, how she had

wanted something else to happen, something special. Michael's visit had been the last thing in the world she had expected. But it had made all of them happy. It was special to give as well as to get, especially to somebody who really needed warmth and shelter and love. And then she thought about Jesus, who came to give his love to everyone in the world. He had been born on Christmas Day in Bethlehem in a stable in the cold – for he too had nowhere else to go. Amy went to sleep that night knowing that this was the happiest Christmas she had ever known.